TINKLE
DIGEST

Greedy Gubbana.....................
The Bear's Advice...19
Atlanta's Race..20-22
Pay Raise..23
Cyber Friend..24-29
You Be the Detective: The Missing Money Box.................................30
The Tiny Turtle...34-37
Unni vs Veeru..38-45
Suppandi: The Case of the Custard Apples......................................46
Defective Detectives: Night Prowlers...52-59
Meet the Squirrel...60-63
Tinkle Times...66
Tail Talk with Maneka Gandhi...68-69
The Moon in the Well..70-71
Tinkle Picture Quiz...72-73
Androcles and the Lion...74-77
The Sun and the Wind..80-81
It Happened to Me...82-83
Tinkle Tells You Why..84-85
The Two Farmers..86-87
Anwar: Saving Energy..88
Prof. Pandu E. G. (Evil Genius)...89-97
Ha... Ha... Hee... Hee... Ho... Ho!!...98

TINKLE DIGEST

EDITOR Rajani Thindiath
ASSISTANT EDITOR Sean D'mello
SUB-EDITOR Aparna Sundaresan
GROUP ART DIRECTOR
Savio Mascarenhas
ARTISTS Archana Amberkar,
Vineet Nair
COLOURING AND LAYOUT Umesh Sarode,
Prasad Sawant
STUDIO COORDINATOR Pranay Bendre
EDITORIAL ASSISTANT Jubel D'Cruz

COVER LAYOUT Pranay Bendre

COO M. Krishna Kiran
BUSINESS HEAD Shriya Ghate
GROUP CREATIVE DIRECTOR Neel Debdutt Paul
MARKETING MANAGER Nitya Subramanian
SUBSCRIPTION EXECUTIVE Kushal Bhandare

PRODUCTION
PRODUCTION HEAD Sagar Sawant
PRODUCTION ASSISTANT Shrikant Wagle

DGM-Legal, Licensing & Digital Publishing
Lalit Sharma

@TinkleDigest

Tinkle Comics Studio

Disclaimer:
In no event will Amar Chitra Katha Pvt. Ltd., be liable for any loss or damage including without limitation, indirect or consequential loss or damage arising from or in connection with the use of Free Gifts/Samples.

ADVERTISING SALES
Sr. Vice President (National)
Eric D'souza +91-9820056421
Assistant Account Director-Print & Online (West)
Rahul Singhania (rahul.singhania@ack-media.com)
Key Account Manager (Mumbai)
Pranuthi Kurma (pranuthi.kurma@ack-media.com)
Deputy General Manager-Print & Online (Delhi)
Raj Mani Patel (rajmani.patel@ack-media.com)
Key Account Manager (Delhi)
Aakansha Deopa (aakansha.deopa@ack-media.com)
Consultant (Delhi)
Jaswinder Gill (jaswinder.gill@ack-media.com)
Sr. Account Director (Bengaluru-South)
S.M. Meenakshi (sm.meenakshi@ack-media.com)
Consultant (Chennai)
Shankar Jayaraman (shankar.j@ack-media.com)
Authorized Representative (Eastern Region)
Jain Enterprises, Kolkata
+91-33-22488257 (bcjain@vsnl.com)
Assistant Manager (Scheduling)
Sandeep Palande (sandeep.palande@ack-media.com)

ADVERTISING ENQUIRIES
advertisingsales@ack-media.com
+91-22-49188811

SALES: sales@ack-media.com

NEWS STAND SALES
Director: Abizar A. Shaikh (abizar@ibhworld.com)
Regional Head: Rajeev Amberkar (rajeev@ibhworld.com)

© **Amar Chitra Katha Pvt. Ltd.,**
Printed & published by Anuraag Agarwal on behalf of Amar Chitra Katha Private Limited, printed at Indigo Press (India) Private Limited, plot no. 1C/716, opp. Dadoji Konddeo Cross Road, between Sussex & Retiwala Industrial Estates, Byculla (E), Mumbai 400027
and published at Amar Chitra Katha Pvt. Ltd., Unit No. 201 & 202, Sumer Plaza, 2nd Floor, Marol Maroshi Road, Andheri (East), Mumbai 400059
Editor: Rajani Thindiath
For Consumer Complaints Contact Tel : +91-22-40497436
Email: customerservice@ack-media.com

Enquiries: contact@ibhworld.com
IBH Books and Magazines Distributors Pvt. Ltd.
Distribution Offices: North – Delhi
East – Kolkata **West** – Mumbai
South – Bengaluru, Chennai,
Hyderabad, Thiruvananthapuram

TINKLE CHATTER!

Suppandi: Hello, guys! Am I late?

Tantri (fuming): No, Suppandi. We've been waiting only 45 minutes for you to show up!

Suppandi: Whoops! Sorry! I was reading the latest issue of *Tinkle Digest* and didn't realize how much time had passed.

Tantri (smirking): It took you so long to read it? Ha! I finished it last week!

Shambu: Hey! I too finished reading the issue today!

Tantri: Sheesh! You two dodos belong together.

Shambu: Speaking of dodos, there are some fantastic animal stories from the *Tinkle* archives in this *Tinkle Digest*. I really liked 'The Tiny Turtle'. That's one smart fellow!

Tantri: He's smart, all right, but not smarter than Professor Pandu E.G. aka Evil Genius. Now, that is a man after my own heart.

Suppandi: I thought Baby Veeru in 'Unni vs Veeru' was smart.

Tantri: Yeah, that baby can teach you a few things. How do you always manage to make a mess?

Suppandi: That's not fair! The Defective Detectives too make a mess of things.

Tantri: Ha! I bet you relate to them the best.

Shambu: Actually, Tantri, I think you relate to them the best, since you also always fumble in the end! Hahahaha!

Tantri: Grrrr!

Shambu: Anyway, I quite enjoyed the puzzles. As they say, 'A puzzle a day keeps the tiger away!'

Tantri & Suppandi: Huh?

Shambu: Yes, so I'm off to finish doing them. If Shanti or anyone else comes looking for me with an assignment, just tell them I'm already occupied. Ta-da! No tiger!

Suppandi: Wow! Shambu, you're so smart!

Tantri: SHEESH!

*Well, dear reader, we hope this issue of Tinkle Digest
also keeps you as occupied as Shambu!*

GREEDY GUBBANNA
— A FOLKTALE FROM KARNATAKA
Script: Subba Rao   Illustrations: M. Mohandas

GUBBANNA AND HIS WIFE, GUBBI LIVED IN A MANGO TREE NEAR A VILLAGE.

ONE DAY AS THEY FLEW OVER THE VILLAGE—

WAH! THIS KHEER IS TASTY!

KHEER? WHAT'S THAT?

KHEER IS A SWEET.

IS IT SWEETER THAN RIPE MANGOES?

WELL... IT HAS A DIFFERENT TASTE.

HAVE YOU TASTED IT?

OF COURSE!

WILL YOU MAKE SOME FOR ME?

I WILL, IF YOU BRING ME SOME MILK, A POT AND A SPOON.

GUBBI GOT BUSY MAKING A FIRE.

SOME TIME LATER —

AH, HERE HE COMES!

CAREFUL! PLACE IT GENTLY ON THE FIRE.

THE POTTER GAVE ME THE POT AND THE SPOON. AND THE MILK-MAN GAVE ME THE MILK.

GOOD. NOW GET ME SOME GRAM.

GUBBANNA FLEW TO THE BIGGEST SHOP IN THE VILLAGE MARKET.

CAN YOU GIVE ME SOME GRAM, SIR?

CERTAINLY!

GUBBANNA COLLECTED THE PACKET OF GRAM AND LEFT.

DO COME BACK IF YOU NEED ANYTHING ELSE.

SOON THE GRAM WAS ADDED TO THE MILK.

IS THE KHEER READY?

NOT YET, DEAR. I NEED SOME JAGGERY.

GUBBANNA FLEW BACK TO THE GROCER FOR THE JAGGERY.

YOU MAY TAKE AS MUCH AS YOU CAN CARRY.

AFTER THE JAGGERY WAS STIRRED INTO THE MILK —

CAN WE HAVE THE KHEER NOW?

BE PATIENT, DEAR. I NEED A FEW CARDAMOMS..

SO AWAY FLEW GUBBANNA TO THE CARDAMOM FIELDS.

HE PICKED A FEW CARDAMOMS AND BROUGHT THEM TO HIS WIFE.

THERE! YOUR KHEER IS READY.

AT LAST!

GUBBANNA GRABBED THE SPOON...

...TOOK OUT A SPOONFUL OF KHEER AND RAISED IT TO HIS BEAK.

WAIT! IT'S TOO HOT.

BUT GREEDY GUBBANNA HAD ALREADY SWALLOWED THE BOILING HOT KHEER.

OW...OW...

OH, DEAR! OH, DEAR! I TOLD YOU TO WAIT!

UGH! YOU CALL THIS TASTY! IT HAS BURNT MY MOUTH!

LISTEN...

BUT GUBBANNA WAS IN NO MOOD TO LISTEN. HE CARRIED THE POT TO THE TANK NEAR BY...

...AND FLUNG IT INTO THE WATER.

SPLASH

WHEN HE WENT BACK, HE WAS SHOCKED TO SEE HIS WIFE ABOUT TO PECK AT THE KHEER THAT WAS STUCK TO THE SPOON.

HEY! ARE YOU MAD?

DO YOU TOO WANT TO BURN YOUR MOUTH?

YOU BURN YOUR MOUTH ONLY IF YOU EAT KHEER THAT IS BOILING HOT.

THIS KHEER IS COLD... AND IS TASTY!

TASTY, DID YOU SAY?

DON'T BE AFRAID. GO AHEAD. EAT IT.

WELL... SINCE YOU SAY SO, I WILL.

THE NEXT MOMENT—

WHY, I'VE NEVER TASTED ANYTHING LIKE THIS BEFORE! IT'S DELICIOUS!

AND YOU COULD HAVE HAD MORE OF IT...

...IF ONLY YOU HADN'T BEEN SO HASTY.

HEY! WHERE ARE YOU GOING?

CAN'T YOU GUESS?

HE FLEW STRAIGHT TO THE TANK.

I MUST HAVE THE REST OF THE KHEER. BUT IT'S ALL MIXED WITH THE WATER IN THE TANK.

NOW THE ONLY WAY TO HAVE THE KHEER IS TO DRINK THE WATER.

GLUG! GLUG!

SO HE DRANK ALL THE WATER IN THE TANK.

GLUG, GLU..G

AH! I'VE DONE IT! NOT A DROP LEFT.

JUST THEN—

HEY! WHAT'S HAPPENING?

IT'S THE WATER ESCAPING! I MUST STOP IT.

HE PICKED UP A FEW STRAWS...

...AND STUFFED THEM INTO HIS MOUTH AND EARS.

THERE! NOW THE WATER CANNOT ESCAPE!

BY THEN IT WAS DARK.

I CAN'T SEE A THING! HOW WILL I GET HOME?

HOWEVER, GUBBANNA MANAGED TO HOP ALONG...

...TILL HE REACHED A COTTAGE.

TUK TUK

AN OLD WOMAN OPENED THE DOOR.

WHAT DO YOU WANT?

I...GLUG ...GLUG...

I'VE LOST MY WAY, GRANDMA, GLUG...GLUG...

YOU POOR THING. COME FOLLOW ME.

SHE TOOK HIM TO THE COWSHED.

YOU CAN SLEEP IN THAT CORNER.

THE COW DIDN'T EVEN LOOK AT HIM. SHE CONTINUED TO MUNCH HER HAY.

AFTER A WHILE —

I'VE EATEN ALL THAT HAY AND I'M STILL HUNGRY.

SO SHE LOOKED AROUND FOR MORE. SUDDENLY —

AH, A STRAW!

NOW I'M THIRSTY. IF ONLY THERE WERE SOME WATER...

THE NEXT MOMENT—

WHAT! WATER! I CAN'T BELIEVE IT!

TODAY IS MY LUCKY DAY!

OR IS IT? OH, GOD! THERE SEEMS TO BE A FLOOD HERE!

GUBBANNA WAS STILL FAST ASLEEP.

SOON THE WATER STARTED FLOWING OUT OF THE COWSHED...

...AND INTO THE COTTAGE.

FLOOD!

WHAT SHALL I DO?

I'LL HAVE TO BE PATIENT AND SIT HERE TILL SOMETHING HAPPENS!

MEANWHILE GUBBI WAS WORRIED ABOUT HER HUSBAND.

I WONDER WHERE HE HAS GONE! I'D BETTER GO AND LOOK FOR HIM.

I DON'T UNDERSTAND! NOT A DROP OF RAIN AND YET THE WHOLE VILLAGE IS FLOODED!

SUDDENLY —

AH! THERE HE IS!

SHE PICKED UP HER HUSBAND...

...ROSE HIGH INTO THE SKY...

...AND TOOK HIM TO THE BRANCH OF A TREE.

ARE YOU ALL RIGHT? PLEASE ANSWER ME.

COCO'S GRAND ROAD TRIP EPISODE V

IN THE FOOTHILLS OF THE CHOCOMALAYAS...

I'VE GOT AN ENTIRE DAY OF TREKKING LINED UP FOR US. YOU GUYS WILL LOVE IT!

I'M SURE WE WILL, DHARUN!

AN ENTIRE DAY OF TREKKING? THAT SOUNDS PAINFUL!

COME ON, SHAMBU! I'M CARRYING AN ENTIRE BAG OF KELLOGG'S CHOCOS TO KEEP US GOING!

IF THAT'S THE CASE, THEN I'M READY TO GO ANYWHERE!

YOU GUYS BETTER BE CAREFUL UP THERE. MAKE SURE YOU GET BACK BEFORE IT GETS DARK!

YES, PEOPLE HAVE SPOTTED THE INFAMOUS YETI ROAMING THE HILLSIDE.

BUT YETIS ARE NOT REAL, RIGHT, COCO?

Y-Y-YETI?

RIGHT! THERE'S NEVER BEEN SCIENTIFIC PROOF OF ITS EXISTENCE.

TELL THAT TO PROFESSOR DHOONDKE. HE WENT HUNTING FOR THE YETI THREE MONTHS BACK AND NO ONE HAS SEEN HIM SINCE.

ON SOME NIGHTS, YOU CAN HEAR IT HOWLING IN THE HILLS.

DON'T WORRY! I'VE TAKEN ALL PRECAUTIONS POSSIBLE, FROM CAMPING SUPPLIES TO GPS TRACKERS!

DON'T FORGET OUR BAG FULL OF CHOCOS!

SOON...

I CAN'T... GO... ON, COCO! YOU... GO AHEAD... WITHOUT... ME!

PANT! PANT!

COME ON, SHAMBU! MY JOB AT THE BACK IS TO MAKE SURE NO ONE GETS LEFT BEHIND!

BESIDES, IN ANOTHER TWO KILOMETRES, WE'LL BE TAKING A CHOCOS BREAK!

WE WILL? WHY DIDN'T YOU SAY SO EARLIER?

CRACK

OH NO! THE YETI!

THAT'S NOT A YETI! THAT SOUNDS LIKE A STORM! WE NEED TO FIND SHELTER, GUYS!

THIS LOOKS LIKE A GOOD SPOT.

COME ON, SHAMBU, HURRY!

THE STUPID RAIN HAS GOT US TRAPPED! THAT YETI IS SURE TO GET US NOW!

CALM DOWN, SHAMBU! THERE IS NO SUCH THING AS YETIS.

HOW ABOUT A BOWL OF KELLOGG'S CHOCOS TO SOOTHE YOUR NERVES, SHAMBU?

YOU ALWAYS KNOW HOW TO CALM ME DOWN, COCO.

MMMM! CHOCOS!

YETI!

YETI? WHERE? WHERE?

WHO'S THERE? SHOW YOURSELF!

WHO AM I? ER... I'M NOT REALLY SURE!

WAIT A MINUTE! YOU'RE PROFESSOR DHOONDKE! THE RESEARCHER WHO WENT MISSING!

I AM? AH, YES, OF COURSE! YOU SEE, I HAD LOST MY MEMORY AFTER HAVING AN ACCIDENT HERE.

I THINK JUST SEEING THE KELLOGG'S CHOCOS HAS JOLTED MY MEMORY BACK! AFTER ALL, ONE CAN NEVER FORGET THE CHOCOLATEY DELICIOUSNESS OF KELLOGG'S CHOCOS!

YOU CAN SAY THAT AGAIN! BURP!

YOU SEE, KELLOGG'S CHOCOS IS MY FAVOURITE BREAKFAST!

HOW ABOUT A BOWL THEN?

THE BEAR'S ADVICE

Script: Luis M. Fernandes · Illustrations: Pradeep Sathe

TWO FRIENDS WERE PASSING THROUGH A JUNGLE.

SUDDENLY—

A BEAR!

RUN!

AHH!

I'VE SPRAINED MY ANKLE. HELP ME!

AND LET THE BEAR ATTACK ME? I AM SORRY.

HERE IT COMES. I'LL HOLD MY BREATH...

...AND PLAY DEAD.

THE BEAR STOPPED NEAR THE MAN, SNIFFED AT HIM...

...AND WENT AWAY.

WHEN IT WAS OUT OF SIGHT—

IT LOOKED AS IF THE BEAR WAS WHISPERING SOMETHING IN YOUR EAR. HA! HA!

IT WAS.

IT TOLD ME — BEWARE OF SELFISH FRIENDS.

Atalanta's Race
—A Greek Tale

Script: Luis M. Fernandes
Illustrations: Pradeep Sathe

ATALANTA WAS THE DAUGHTER OF THE KING OF GREECE. SHE HAD AGREED TO MARRY ANY MAN WHO COULD BEAT HER IN A RACE.

MANY MEN TRIED, BUT FAILED.

SHE IS AS SWIFT AS A DEER.

ONE DAY A YOUNG MAN NAMED MILANION CAME TO THE PALACE.

I WISH TO RUN AGAINST THE PRINCESS.

GO BACK, SON.

YOU CANNOT HOPE TO BEAT ATALANTA. SHE IS THE FASTEST RUNNER IN THE WORLD.

I AM A GOOD RUNNER MYSELF.

DO YOU KNOW WHAT HAPPENS TO THE LOSER? HE IS PUT TO DEATH.

I KNOW. I AM NOT AFRAID.

THEN COME BACK TOMORROW FOR THE RACE.

THE NEXT DAY AT THE STARTING POINT—

HE'S SO HANDSOME AND HE SEEMS SO SURE OF HIMSELF.

BUT THE POOR FELLOW DOESN'T HAVE A CHANCE.

THE RACE BEGAN. ATALANTA SPED AWAY.

SHE CAN CERTAINLY RUN FAST.

IT'S TIME TO THROW THE FIRST ONE.

A GOLDEN APPLE!

SHE IS CHASING THE APPLE... JUST AS I EXPECTED.

AND NOW I AM AHEAD OF HER.

BUT IT DID NOT TAKE THE PRINCESS LONG TO OVERTAKE THE YOUTH. THEN HE THREW ANOTHER APPLE AND SHE WENT AFTER THAT ONE TOO.

BUT A LITTLE LATER —

SHE HAS OVERTAKEN ME AGAIN.

THE WINNING POST IS IN SIGHT. I'LL THROW MY LAST APPLE.

ANOTHER ONE.

BY THE TIME ATALANTA PICKED UP THE APPLE...

...AND RAN BACK, MILANION HAD FINISHED THE RACE.

HE HAS WON!

TRUE TO HER WORD, ATALANTA MARRIED THE YOUTH AND THEY LIVED HAPPILY EVER AFTER.

PAY RAISE

Readers' Choice

Based on a story sent by:

Sanket J. Ullal,
7, New Salubhai Bldg,
Uthalsar Road,
Thane (W) - 400 601.

Illustrations:
Nikhil Salvi

GIRDHARI HAD BEEN WORKING AT SETH CHANDU'S SHOP FOR NEARLY TWENTY YEARS.

YOU MUST TALK OF A RAISE NOW. YOUR WAGES CAN NO LONGER SUPPORT US.

BUT WHAT IF HE GETS ANGRY?

BE TACTFUL! CHOOSE A TIME WHEN SETHJI IS IN A GOOD MOOD.

ALL RIGHT, I WILL TRY.

ONE AFTERNOON, SETHJI SEEMED TO BE IN A GOOD MOOD AND GIRDHARI DECIDED TO TRY HIS LUCK.

WHAT IS IT, GIRDHARI?

SETHJI, I... I HAVE WORKED HERE FOR MORE THAN TWENTY YEARS...

...MY HAIR HAS TURNED GREY AND YET....

OH, IS THAT IT? HERE, TAKE THIS TEN-RUPEE NOTE...

...GO TO KALLU RAM, HE USES THE BEST DYE. YOU WILL NOT LOOK A DAY OLDER THAN FIFTY!

GULP!

CYBER FRIEND

3rd Prize 16th Tinkle Original Story Contest

Story: Rajee Raman
Script: Ashwini Falnikar
Art: Crimson Studio
Letters: Prasad Sawant

FOR SUNIL'S 15TH BIRTHDAY, HIS PARENTS HAD ORGANISED A GRAND PARTY BUT HIS HEART WAS ELSEWHERE –

KARTHIK, WILL YOU MEET ME TOMORROW?

TAP TAP TAP

AS HE WAITED FOR A REPLY, THE EVENTS OF THE PAST YEAR FLASHED BEFORE HIS EYES.

A YEAR AGO –

WHISHKYAAN
VEEEEEEE
PHUPP
DHAMM!

SUNIL, STOP IT, PLEASE! I AM WORKING HERE.

THERE IT GOES!

YOU GUYS ARE ALWAYS WORKING! DOES THAT MEAN I SHOULD NEVER PLAY?

SUNIL, COME DOWN. WE NEED TO TALK TO YOU.

YOUR TEACHER CALLED MOM AND SAID YOU HAD TO BE PUSHED PAST THE 'PASS LEVEL'. IS THAT RIGHT?

YEAH...

SHE WANTS TO MEET ME. IS THERE A PROBLEM? BECAUSE I HAVE AN IMPORTANT MEETING TOMORROW.

THERE IS NO NEED.

YES, THERE **IS A NEED** TO WORRY! YOU ATTEND TUITIONS, GO TO THE BEST SCHOOL IN THE CITY, AND THESE ARE YOUR GRADES?

OH STOP IT...

WHAT ABOUT YOUR CAREER? HAVE YOU...

CRASH!

SUNIL!

HE IS GETTING MORE DIFFICULT BY THE DAY.

THIS IS THE PROBLEM WITH HAVING TWO HIGH-ACHIEVERS FOR PARENTS. NAG! NAG! NAG!

HIS POOR PERFORMANCE IN SCHOOL AND IRRITABLE MOOD HAD LEFT HIM FRIENDLESS. SO HE SPENT HOURS IN HIS FAVOURITE CHAT ROOM.

CHATTER BUG

TING

Karthik: Hi, I am Karthik.

Sun: I am Sunil. I live in Chennai…

Karthik: Chennai? Same here! What a beautiful city ☺

SUNIL EASILY CONNECTED WITH KARTHIK AND WAS SOON POURING OUT HIS WOES –

Sun: My parents are forever busy. They want me to be like them but I have other dreams!

Karthik: You are their only son. They are bound to have dreams for you.

Sun: But their constant advising is so annoying! I just avoid talking to them.

Karthik: That must hurt them...

Sun: So… what should I do?

Karthik: Show them you care! Maybe start by making a cup of tea for your mom when she's back from work…

Sun: Hmmm... I'll try that.

THAT EVENING –

MOM, YOU MUST BE TIRED.

THANKS, SON.

UMM.... HOW WAS YOUR DAY?

OH, GOOD, BUT YOU TELL ME ABOUT YOURS...

THIS SMALL INCIDENT BROKE THE ICE.

SO YOU LIKE PHOTOGRAPHY? LIKE DAD?

I GUESS SO. I DID WELL ON THE SCHOOL ASSIGNMENT.

WHEN DAD HAD TIME, HE WOULD JOIN IN –

LET ME SHOW YOU A TRICK.

IN SPITE OF BUSY SCHEDULES, THEY MADE TIME FOR EACH OTHER –

HAHAHA...

OH, THAT'S SO FUNNY...

MEANWHILE SUNIL SHARED EVERYTHING WITH KARTHIK –

Sun: School is hectic. Work never gets over.

Karthik: You need to learn time management. Plan ahead.☺

I hate to admit it, but your tips always work ☺

SUNIL TRIED HIS BEST AND IT SHOWED. AT SCHOOL –

YOU DID VERY WELL, SUNIL!

THANKS, BUT I WILL PREPARE BETTER NEXT TIME.

THE SITUATION AT SCHOOL IMPROVED, AND SLOWLY SUNIL WON BACK HIS CONFIDENCE –

DAD, I'VE THOUGHT ABOUT A CAREER OPTION...

GO ON...

UMM... I WANT TO TAKE UP ENGLISH LITERATURE AND BECOME A WRITER, LIKE UNCLE VIJAY.

I AM NOT SURPRISED, SON. YOU HAVE ALWAYS WRITTEN WELL. WE WILL GO TO VIJAY'S THIS SUNDAY.

BACK TO THE DAY BEFORE HIS BIRTHDAY –

KARTHIK, YOU DID IT AGAIN!

I HOPE KARTHIK AGREES TO MEET ME...

THE VISIT TO UNCLE VIJAY'S PROVED TO BE FRUITFUL.

ting

Karthik: I would love to meet you! How about Natesan Park at 4.30 pm?

Sun: Done! ☺ But how will I recognize you?

Karthik: I'll be wearing a yellow T-shirt and blue jeans.

Sun: Done!

THE NEXT DAY –

THATHA* – YOU?!

YES, MY BOY! KARTHIK AT YOUR SERVICE!

BUT... BUT, WHY...?

*TAMIL FOR GRANDFATHER

The Missing Money Box

"I'm going to ace this project," thought 12-year-old Sarah contentedly as she placed some more money in the already full cash box of her fresh fruit juice stall. One week had passed and her stall, which she had set up as part of her Social Studies class project, had done so well that many of her classmates had been envious.

That afternoon, Mrs. Jain walked up to Sarah and said, "Hello, dearie! Isn't this the last day of your project?"

Sarah grinned, "Yes, Mrs. Jain." "Oh well," Mrs. Jain sighed disappointedly, "I will miss the yummy juices you serve. So, what do you have for me today?"

"There's apple, orange, sweet lime and blackberry. What would you like?" Sarah asked, smiling.

"I'll have the blackberry juice. But could you please give me a tissue? Last time, I had spilled some on my saree and it had left a designer stain I could certainly do without," said Mrs. Jain wryly.

As Sarah handed her a glass of juice, she spotted her classmates, Radha and Manish.

"Hey guys! What brings you here? How is business?" Sarah asked them brightly.

"Good. I just need something to drink before I go on my next cookie-sale trip," replied Radha.

"And I just took a break from my car wash. Not too many people want to get their cars cleaned in the afternoon," replied Manish.

"You didn't give me that tissue, dearie," Mrs. Jain reminded Sarah

gently.

"Oh, I'm sorry. I'll have to get tissues from inside... Would you please look after the stall while I fetch them, Aunty?" asked an apologetic Sarah as she disappeared into her house.

When she returned, she saw that her stall was unattended. Mrs. Jain was deep in conversation with another lady while Radha and Manish were idling on the lawn. She hurriedly handed Mrs. Jain a couple of tissues and returned to her place behind the counter.

"An orange juice, please," ordered the girl at the head of the queue, handing Sarah a 100-rupee note. Sarah reached for her cash box under the counter to get change and gasped. The box was gone and so was all the money she had earned in the past week.

"Mrs. Jain," she called out, "have you seen my cash box? It's missing!"

The lady looked horrified and then replied embarrassedly, "I'm so sorry, Sarah. I became so engrossed in talk that I completely forgot to pay attention to your stall. I have no idea what happened to

your money."

"No problem, Aunty," sighed Sarah and called out to Radha and Manish, "You guys! Did you see someone take my money box?"

"Nope," answered Manish as he and Radha walked over to Sarah. "I was too busy downing blackberry juice. I hope you don't mind that I helped myself to some while you were gone."

"I didn't see anyone either. I was selling cookies to some of your customers in the queue. I think I've made enough to get the highest grade in the project," said Radha complacently.

"Ha! My car wash will beat you hands down, Miss cookie-seller," scoffed Manish.

"Dream on, washer boy!" said Radha, rolling her eyes.

Manish sneered and stuck out his tongue at her. Radha stuck hers right back at him.

"All right, guys. Enough with this childish nonsense," said Sarah, impatiently. "Now Manish, will you please return my cash box?"

How did Sarah know it was Manish who had taken the box?

Answer : Like Mrs. Jain had pointed out, blackberry juice left a stain due to its dark purple colour. When Manish stuck his tongue out at Radha, Sarah noticed that his tongue was unstained (refer picture). Thus he was lying when he said that he'd been busy drinking blackberry juice while Sarah was gone. That's how Sarah inferred that he'd taken the money.

Create your masterpiece based on the themes below and you could WIN AMAZING PRIZES!

Group A: Upto 4 years
Theme: "My Toy"

Group B: Standards I and II
Theme: "My Favourite Park"

Group C: Standards III and IV
Theme: "My Hobbies"

Group D: Standards V and VI
Theme: "City Traffic"

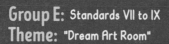

Group E: Standards VII to IX
Theme: "Dream Art Room"

Group F: Standards X to XII
Theme: "The World in My Eyes"

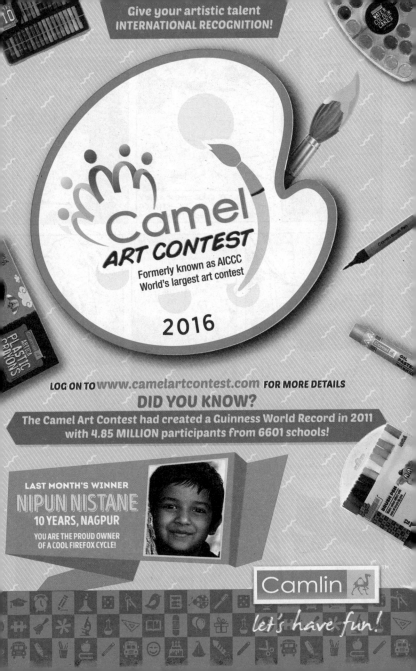

THE TINY TURTLE

AN AFRICAN FOLK TALE

Script: Subba Rao
Illustrations: M. Mohandas

THERE ONCE LIVED A TINY TURTLE ON THE BANK OF THE CONGO RIVER.

HE OFTEN WANDERED INTO THE FOREST NEAR BY.

ONE DAY —

OH! OH! WHAT'S THAT?

THE FRIGHTENED TURTLE SHRANK INTO ITS SHELL.

DID I GIVE YOU A SCARE, TINY TURTLE? HA! HA! HA!

OH! IT'S THAT BOASTFUL ELEPHANT!

DON'T LAUGH, MY FRIEND. I MAY BE SMALLER THAN YOU. BUT I'M AS STRONG AS YOU.

AS STRONG AS ME? HO! HO! HO!

DON'T LAUGH. I CAN PROVE IT TO YOU.

LET'S HAVE A TUG-OF-WAR TOMORROW.

HO! HO! HO! ALL RIGHT, TINY TURTLE. WE'LL DO AS YOU SAY.

THE TURTLE THEN WENT BACK TO THE RIVER BANK.

WAKE UP, HIPPO! I HAVE NEWS FOR YOU.

WHO DARES DISTURB MY SLEEP!

IT'S YOU! GO AWAY BEFORE I EAT YOU UP!

YOU SAY THAT BECAUSE I'M MUCH SMALLER THAN YOU. BUT I'M AS STRONG AS YOU.

HO! HO! HO!

DON'T LAUGH! LET'S HAVE A TUG-OF-WAR TOMORROW AND LET'S SEE WHO WINS.

ALL RIGHT! ALL RIGHT!

THE NEXT MORNING —

HERE TAKE THIS END OF THE ROPE, HIPPO.

NOW, WAIT TILL I REACH THE EDGE OF THE FOREST WITH THIS END AND CALL OUT TO YOU TO START TUGGING.

HURRY UP.

I MIGHT AS WELL HAVE A NAP WHILE I'M WAITING.

THE TURTLE THEN WENT TO THE ELEPHANT.

HERE IS THE ROPE.

NOW WAIT TILL I GO TO THE BANK OF THE RIVER AND PICK UP THE OTHER END OF THE ROPE.

ALL RIGHT, TINY TURTLE! BUT BE QUICK!

THE TURTLE WALKED TOWARDS THE RIVER.

AH! I'LL STAY HERE. NOW THE FUN BEGINS.

COME ON, START TUGGING.

AT THE EDGE OF THE FOREST —

AT THE BANK OF THE RIVER —

HEY! WHAT'S HAPPENING?

THIS TURTLE IS STRONGER THAN I THOUGHT.

JUST AS I THOUGHT. I'LL WIN!

HEY! WHAT'S THIS? I CAN'T BELIEVE IT.

THUS THE TUG-OF-WAR CONTINUED.

ALL DAY LONG THE TWO MIGHTY ANIMALS TUGGED AND TUGGED. WHEN IT WAS EVENING BOTH DROPPED THE ROPE AT THE SAME TIME.

NOW DO YOU AGREE THAT I AM STRONGER THAN YOU?

NEITHER THE ELEPHANT NOR THE HIPPOPOTAMUS HAD THE ENERGY TO ANSWER HIM. BUT NEVER AGAIN DID THE TWO LAUGH AT THE TURTLE.

UNNI VS VEERU

Based on a story sent by Seema Bokkasam

Script: Rajani Thindiath
Illustrator: Nikhil Salvi
Colourist: Umesh Sarode
Letterer: Pranay Bendre

UNNI'S COMING.

OH NO! NOT AGAIN!

WHO'S UNNI?

WELL... HE'S YOUR FATHER'S COUSIN. HE WAS HERE LAST WHEN YOU WERE VEERU'S AGE.

AND WHAT A VISIT THAT WAS! TOILETRIES WENT MISSING...

...FOOD DISAPPEARED FROM THE FRIDGE OVERNIGHT...

...ANY SPARE CHANGE WE LEFT LYING AROUND WAS 'ORPHANED' ACCORDING TO UNNI!

AND HE WOULD 'ADOPT' IT FROM THE GOODNESS OF HIS HEART!

THE PEST! I'M DREADING WHAT HE'LL PILFER DURING THIS VISIT.

LET'S JUST BE CAREFUL AND NOT LEAVE THINGS LYING AROUND.

FAT CHANCE WITH OUR LITTLE TORNADO AROUND!

VEERU! KEEP YOUR STICKY HANDS OFF MY GAMES!

CRASH!

UNNI ARRIVED WITH A BANG...

BANG!

HELLO EVERYONE!

YOU DIDN'T TELL US HE WAS LOUD TOO. I DON'T LIKE HIM ALREADY.

HUSH!

HEHE... AND THIS MUST BE VEERU.

WAAAH!

VEERU DOESN'T LIKE HIM EITHER. UNCLE UNNI HAD BETTER WATCH OUT.

WAAAAAAH!

AAAH... WELL... I HAD BETTER FRESHEN UP.

THE NEXT MORNING —

I CAN'T FIND THE BUNCH OF TEN RUPEE NOTES I'D LEFT ON THE TABLE...

UNNI, DID YOU FILCH THE TENNERS I'D LEFT ON THE TABLE?

FILCH THEM?! I'M NOT SOME COMMON THIEF! I SIMPLY ADOPTED THEM!

HMPH! WELL UN-ADOPT THEM! I NEED THE CHANGE FOR THE RICKSHAW.

SORRY! FINDERS KEEPERS!

GRRRR!

UNNI, DO YOU HAVE MY PERFUME? I'D FORGOTTEN TO TAKE IT FROM THE GUEST ROOM BUT...

AND MY NEW VIDEO GAME! IT'S MISSING TOO!

WHAT IS THIS? A **CONSPIRACY**?! YOU'RE TREATING ME LIKE A COMMON CRIMINAL! I WON'T STAND IT!

I'M LEAVING RIGHT NOWWWWW!

VEEERU!

MOM, DAD, LOOK! UNCLE UNNI'S BAG!

ARE YOU ALL RIGHT?

MY PERFUME!

MY GAME!

DUCK! DUCK!

SOME TIME LATER —

EVERYONE MUST BE ASLEEP NOW. NOW'S THE TIME FOR MY NIGHT RAID.

I WONDER WHAT TO START WITH... THE GULAB JAMUN, THE KHEER, THE ICE CREAM OR THE CHOCOLATES...

I'LL START WITH...

ULP!

WAAAAH!

UNNI!

I... AH... I JUST CAME IN FOR A GLASS OF WATER.

I BET!

HOW COME VEERU'S NOT ASLEEP?

THAT'S HIS ROUTINE. HE GOES TO SLEEP IN THE EVENING AND THEN REMAINS AWAKE HALF THE NIGHT!

OH NO! THERE GOES MY CHANCE!

WELL, I'LL GET BACK TO BED...

SNOORRRRE! SNOORRE!

(SNIFF! SNIFF!) ACCHHOO!

HAHAHAHA!

WHAT?! WHAT?

VEEERU!

I'M SORRY, UNNI. I'D JUST DOZED OFF...

HUMPH!

BUT UNNI COULD NOT SLEEP THAT NIGHT. VEERU KEPT HIM UP WITH HIS ANTICS —

CLANG! CLANG! CLANG!

WHY DID I COME HERE!

OW! OW!

NEXT MORNING —

WHAT'S MISSING TODAY?

NOT A THING!

I'M SURPRISED. WHAT HAPPENED TO UNNI?

VEERU HAPPENED! VEERU KEPT HIM UP ALL NIGHT.

I TOLD YOU. VEERU DIDN'T LIKE BEING BLAMED FOR GETTING OUR THINGS IN UNCLE'S BAG!

BUT WHERE IS UNNI?

I'VE NOT SEEN HIM.

NEITHER HAVE I!

LOOK HERE:

"DEAR DEEPAK, I GOT THE FEELING THAT VEERU HAS TAKEN AN INTENSE DISLIKE TO ME. I'VE NEVER SPENT SUCH A TORTUROUS NIGHT...

...DON'T WORRY, I'LL KEEP IN TOUCH... BY PHONE! BYE, UNNI"

GOD BLESS VEERU!

THE CASE OF THE CUSTARD APPLES

A Suppandi Tale

Readers' Choice

Based on a story sent by:

Aditya A. Malshe

Illustrations:
Archana Amberkar

SUPPANDI'S NEW MASTER WAS A CHEF.

SUPPANDI, GET TWO KILOS OF CUSTARD APPLES FROM THE MARKET.

YES, MASTER.

AT THE MARKET –

COULD I HAVE TWO KILOS OF CUSTARD APPLES, PLEASE?

SORRY, WE ARE OUT OF CUSTARD APPLES.

MASTER IS GOING TO BE VERY PLEASED WITH ME.

AT LAST, AFTER TWO HOURS –

SUPPANDI! WHAT ON EARTH TOOK YOU SO LONG? THE MARKET IS ONLY 15 MINUTES AWAY.

WELL, MASTER, THEY DIDN'T HAVE ANY CUSTARD APPLES AT THE MARKET ...

PUFF!

... SO I WENT TO THE DAIRY, BOUGHT SOME CUSTARD AND THEN BOUGHT APPLES FROM THE MARKET. WE CAN MAKE THE CUSTARD APPLES AT HOME.

SIGH!

AN IDIOMATIC TALE

SUPPANDI! WHAT HAVE YOU DONE!

S... S... SORRY, SIR! IT WAS AN ACCIDENT!

SIGH! IT'S FINE. THERE'S NO USE CRYING OVER SPILT MILK NOW.

MILK? WHO SPILLED MILK?

IT'S AN IDIOM, SUPPANDI! ANYWAY, WHAT ARE WE GOING TO DO ABOUT THESE PAPERS NOW?

I DID MAKE ANOTHER SET OF COPIES. WILL THAT HELP?

YOU DID? PERFECT, SUPPANDI! YOU'VE HIT THE NAIL ON THE HEAD!

I HIT A NAIL ON SOMEONE'S HEAD? WHEN DID I DO THAT, SIR?

GO HOME AND LEARN YOUR IDIOMS, SUPPANDI!

UM, I HAVE NO IDEA WHAT IDIOMS ARE! DO YOU THINK YOU GUYS CAN HELP ME LEARN ABOUT IDIOMS?

Oh Suppandi! An idiom is just a phrase that has a deeper meaning rather than the obvious one.

Q1. Can you guess the idioms from the images below?

_____

Q2. What is your favourite idiom and why?

_____

_____

Answer both questions using your

Camlin Exam 2.0 mm Mechanical Pencil!

Then, send us an image of the completed contest page via:

✉ camlinwritercontest@ack-media.com   OR   📷 tinkleonline.com/camlinwritercontest

OR   💬 whatsapp it to 7666112255

Dear Readers,

Four years ago, *Tinkle Digest* broke away from its original classic avatar to turn into a separate magazine. Without our loyal readers, we would never have made it this far—50 issues of original stories and fascinating characters that **you** helped create. We hope you enjoyed reading those stories just as much as we did in writing and illustrating them. Thank you for supporting us!

From last month, based on popular demand, *Tinkle Digest* once again became a collection of classic *Tinkle* stories. You are now receiving 100 pages of *Tinkle*'s best stories and features from the last 35 years!

Every month, there will be a mix of folk tales, jokes, puzzles, science features, stories from history, and even the earliest escapades of our beloved Tinkle Toons Suppandi, Shikari Shambu and Tantri the Mantri that have since become rare finds. We will also bring you Uncle Pai's beloved stories as well as his hand-picked tales from our vast collection. Rest assured, there will never be a dull moment in these pages!

Tinkle Digest has gotten a makeover, but it is still the action-packed magazine you love. We are excited to bring you its new avatar and hope you are too to receive it. Do write to us on **digest.editor@ack-media.com** and let us know your thoughts on the new *Tinkle Digest*.

Love,
Team Tinkle

Defective Detectives
NIGHT PROWLERS

Writer: Rajani Thindiath
Art: Abhijeet Kini
Letterer: Pranay Bendre

PARENTS ASLEEP?

CHECK! (CHOMP... CHOMP)

SAM?

(CHOMP... CHOMP) SNORING LOUD ENOUGH TO WAKE THE DEAD.

ALL CLEAR, AGENT SHRIEKING BAT?

(CHOMP... GULP) ALL CLEAR, AGENT HOWLING WOLF.

GREAT! I LOVE THE NIGHT. IT'S JUST THE RIGHT TIME TO HUNT CRIMINALS.

TRUE (CHOMP... CHOMP)

AGENT SHRIEKING BAT, IF YOU CAN STOP MUNCHING ON THOSE PEANUTS FOR A MINUTE AND TAKE A...

AAAARGH!

YIKES!

SCREEECH!

WHO ARE YOU?

WHO ARE YOU!

I ASKED FIRST!

HE'S RIGHT, AGENT SHRIEKING BAT.

AGENT? AS IN YOU ARE SOME KIND OF DETECTIVES!

IS HE MAKING FUN OF US?

NOW LOOK HERE, MISTER...

OH, I'M SO **GLAD** I MET YOU! YOU SEE, I'M PHOOLYU, A SPY FOR OUR COUNTRY — HERE'S MY ID. I'VE BEEN TRYING TO GET THESE **TOP-SECRET** DOCUMENTS TO HEADQUARTERS.

WOW, **REALLY?!** GLAD TO MEET YOU, MR. PHOOLYU!

GREAT! BECAUSE, YOU SEE, I HAVE **ENEMY AGENTS** ON MY TAIL! I HAVE BEEN DODGING THEM ALL **NIGHT**!

BUT YOU TWO COULD HELP ME!

ANYTHING FOR THE COUNTRY!

GOOD! TAKE THESE DOCUMENTS. THEY WON'T SUSPECT YOU. HAND THEM TO ME IN AN HOUR'S TIME OUTSIDE JOGGER'S PARK.

BUT STAY LOW. THE ENEMY AGENT IS DISGUISED AS A COP THOUGH HE HAS THIS RATHER FUNNY WALRUS MOUSTACHE.

CHILL, MAN! THEY ARE SAFE WITH US.

AS SOON AS MR. PHOOLYU LEFT —

AGENT HOWLING WOLF, THE COP!

WALRUS MOUSTACHE! **DUCK**!

?!

I DON'T SEE HIM...

I THINK WE'VE LOST HIM, AGENT SHRIEKING BAT!

GOTCHA!

AT THE POLICE STATION, AFTER THE BOYS' PARENTS WERE SUMMONED —

WHAT IN THE WORLD IS HAPPENING, RAVI?! WHY ARE WE HERE?

JUST A MINUTE, SIR. BOYS, WOULD YOU CARE TO EXPLAIN WHY YOU WERE RUNNING AROUND WITH THESE DOCUMENTS?

THEY ARE **TOP-SECRET** DOCUMENTS, INSPECTOR!

I KNOW THAT! BUT WHAT WERE **YOU** DOING WITH THEM?

QUIET! 'MR. FOOL YOU' **IS** THE ENEMY AGENT WHO **STOLE** THOSE DOCUMENTS FROM HEADQUARTERS! AND MY MEN HAD BEEN TRYING TO GET THEM BACK!

WHAT?! B-BUT HE SHOWED US HIS ID!

THIS ONE PERHAPS? AT LEAST THIS IS THE ONLY ONE HE WAS CARRYING WHEN WE CAUGHT HIM...

...TRYING TO CLIMB THE FENCE TO GET INTO JOGGER'S PARK! THE FOOL, THE GATE WAS WIDE OPEN!

STAR... CIRCUS!

STAR CIRCUS

I DISOWN MY SON!

SHEESH! WE DISOWN OURSELVES!

MEET THE SQUIRREL

Based on the material provided by Nandini Deshmukh

Script: Lopamudra

Illustrations: Pradeep Sathe

HAVE YOU EVER WATCHED A SQUIRREL?

ONE LEAP TAKES HIM ALMOST FOUR FEET UP THE TRUNK OF A TREE. WILL HE SLIP AND FALL?

NOT WITH SUCH SHARP CLAWS!

ISN'T HE CUTE NOW NIBBLING AWAY AT THE MANGO...

...NOW GRINDING HIS SHARP FRONT TEETH?

IF HE DOES NOT DO IT, THESE TEETH WILL GROW LONGER THAN HIS BUSHY TAIL!

WHAT A NASTY THING TO DO!

OUR SQUIRREL'S EYES ARE HALF-CLOSED AND HE IS HANGING UPSIDE DOWN. IS HE...DEAD?

HEY! WHAT IS THIS BOY UP TO? HE'S OUT TO HIT OUR SQUIRREL!

THE NAUGHTY BOY DOES NOT CARE. HE WANTS A SQUIRREL, DEAD OR ALIVE, TO SHOW OFF TO HIS FRIENDS.

BUT WHEN THE NAUGHTY BOY IS ABOUT TO CATCH HIM, OUR FRIEND JUMPS TO SAFETY USING HIS TAIL AS A PARACHUTE!

HE WAS ONLY PRETENDING TO BE DEAD! A TRICK HE USES WHEN AN ENEMY IS AFTER HIM!

HERE HE COMES WITH HIS FRIENDS.

SUDDENLY THEY COME TO A HALT. THAT PEEPING CALL! IT'S MISS SQUIRREL TELLING THEM THAT SHE IS LOOKING FOR A MATE. BUT WHICH OF THEM WILL SHE ACCEPT?

THE STRONGEST, OF COURSE. SO OUR FRIENDS BEGIN TO PROVE THEIR STRENGTH.

WELL DONE! OUR OLD FRIEND IS THE WINNER! AND HERE HE IS BY HER SIDE.

WHAT A FIGHT! COME ON! KEEP IT UP!

BUT AFTER ALL THAT FUSS, HE LIVES WITH MRS. SQUIRREL FOR ONLY A DAY! THEN HE'S OFF.

SHE LOVES BIRDS' EGGS! ARE THERE ANY IN HERE?

DOES MRS. SQUIRREL MIND? NOT ONE BIT. SHE CAN LOOK AFTER HERSELF AND THE BABIES SHE'LL HAVE! THERE SHE GOES LOOKING FOR FOOD.

NO? BAD LUCK!

WELL, SHE'LL FIND HERSELF SOME NUTS OR BERRIES. MM-M-M!

GO AHEAD, MRS. SQUIRREL. HAVE YOUR FILL! YOU'RE GOING TO BE A MOTHER SOON! YOU MUST TAKE CARE OF YOURSELF!

JUICY, FRESH BERRIES! SO MANY OF THEM!

NOW WHAT IS SHE UP TO? O-O-OH! SHE'S GOING TO BUILD A NEST.

SEE HOW HARD SHE WORKS! A LITTLE JUTE AND··· WHAT'S THAT?

SHE IS PULLING OFF HAIR FROM HER OWN TAIL! WELL! WELL! WHAT WON'T A MOTHER DO, EVEN A SQUIRREL MOTHER, TO MAKE A WARM HOME FOR HER CHILDREN!

MY WORD! WHAT A BEAUTIFUL NEST! WITHIN 45 DAYS SHE'LL HAVE THREE OR FOUR BABIES IN IT.

LIKE THESE IN THIS NEST. UGH! DID YOU CALL THEM BEAUTIFUL? LOOK AT THEM! THEY'RE UGLY! THEIR EARS ALL FOLDED IN, THEIR EYES CLOSED. CAN SUCH UGLY CREATURES BE THE CHILDREN OF BEAUTIFUL, BRIGHT-EYED MOTHER SQUIRREL?

PATIENCE, MY FRIEND. SEVEN DAYS LATER THEIR EARS WILL STRAIGHTEN OUT.

A FORTNIGHT AFTER THAT THEIR EYES WILL OPEN.

AND YET A FORTNIGHT LATER, THEIR BODIES WILL BE COVERED WITH HAIR...

...LIKE THESE LITTLE ONES OUT HERE TRYING TO HUNT FOR THEIR OWN FOOD.

YOU HAVE MET THE PALM-SQUIRREL. HERE ARE SOME OF THE OTHER SQUIRRELS WE HAVE IN OUR COUNTRY.

THE FLYING SQUIRREL

THE INDIAN GIANT SQUIRREL

THE HIMALAYAN SQUIRREL

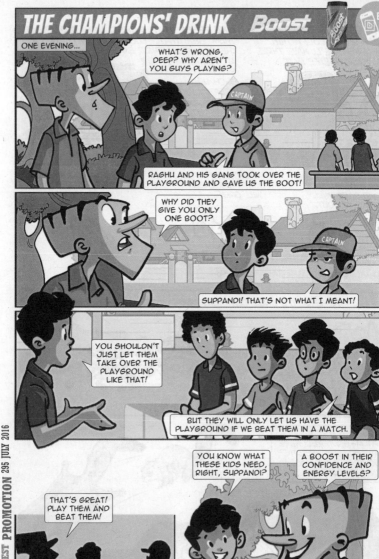

OVER THE NEXT FEW DAYS, DEEP AND HIS TEAM PRACTISE HARD.

GREAT PRACTICE TODAY, GUYS! KEEP IT UP AND REMEMBER TO DRINK BOOST! IT'S WHAT CHAMPIONS DRINK!

SOON, DEEP AND HIS TEAM ARE READY TO TAKE ON THE OLDER BOYS...

TWO BALLS LEFT. FOUR RUNS TO WIN. GOT TO HIT THE NEXT BALL OUT OF THE PARK!

DEEP TIMES HIS SHOT AND SWINGS...

THWACK!

IT'S A SIX!

WE WON!

THAT WAS SOME PERFORMANCE, DEEP. YOU GUYS PLAY AT TOTALLY ANOTHER LEVEL! WHAT'S YOUR SECRET?

BOOST IS THE SECRET OF OUR ENERGY!

TINKLE TIMES

HEADLINES FROM YESTERYEARS

Lab Under the Sea (Florida)

James Lindholm is a biologist who is studying undersea life. His home, for days, has been the 12-metre long sea lab, Aquarius, which stations itself approximately 19 metres under the water's surface.

Scientists and researchers spend up to 10 days in Aquarius conducting a variety of experiments. These could range from studies on water pollution to naval rescue operations and astronaut training. The lab has enough space for experiments, for eating, and six bunks to sleep in. The food is either boiled or microwaved and includes fruits and cheese.

A generator and a pump, stationed in a buoy that floats on the surface, provide Aquarius with electricity and air. The entire mission is controlled from a nearby place called Key Largo.

Policeboy at 15 (Mumbai)

Vijay Hadawale is a member of the Mumbai Police Force. But what makes him unique is that he is only 15 years old! Vijay is one of the 62 *bal sipahis*, who form the teen brigade of the Mumbai City Police. Their job is to work for senior ranking police officers.

Vijay got this job when his father who was a head constable died of a heart attack while on duty. With his salary of Rs 4,261 he supports his mother and two school-going siblings. He is also studying for his Class XI after having scored 63% in the 10th standard exam.

Vijay wants to study and take the exam for a Sub-Inspector's job so that he can become one and chase criminals! May your dream come true, Vijay.

Detective Maths (U. S. A.)

Paintings by famous artists sell for lakhs of rupees. Sometimes, people make imitations of well-known paintings and sell them. This is called forgery. Some forgeries are so well done that it is difficult to detect them.

Now researchers are using mathematics to tell the real from the fake. They start with a digital image of the painting and use a mathematical technique known as wavelet decomposition. This breaks up the image into smaller, more basic images. In a painting when these images are analysed, experts can find out the texture of an artist's brush strokes.

When someone tries to copy a master artist, the brush strokes would be different. The master could have smooth strokes and the imitator jerky strokes. Through the wavelet decomposition technique, experts can find out the real from the false.

Maths does have many uses!

Swimming Champ (Faridabad)

Tinkle reader, Nikita Bali, wrote in from Faridabad, U.P., and told us that she had won the District Level Championship in swimming. In all she had won four gold medals, one silver and one bronze.

Nikita hopes to become a National Champion some day. Great going, Nikita! We are proud of you!

TAIL TALK
WITH MANEKA GANDHI

We share our planet with almost 30 million other species of life forms. And there is so much that we need to know about them.

Mrs. **Maneka Gandhi** is a renowned activist-politician who has worked tirelessly for animal welfare and the environment.

Why do my cats tear the leaves off my house plants? They don't eat them.

I think your cats enjoy this! They are just playing. You could try moving your plants to a higher position or a room where your cats can't reach. Or try and find toys that will keep your cats amused for long periods of time. This may not stop them from doing it but will probably reduce the damage.

My neighbours have a dog. He is so skinny it's pitiful. He comes to my house every day and gobbles up all the food I can find to feed him, even lettuce. I am afraid that he is going hungry and I can't deal with this animal. Whom should I call and what can I do?
Madanpal Rathi, Noida

Please call your local animal welfare group and ask that they send out an investigator. No dog should suffer or starve. It could be that the neighbour is feeding the dog but it may have a medical problem that needs attention. It's important that your neighbour knows that they cannot let a dog go hungry or neglect any medical treatment. If the investigator finds that the dog is not taken care of properly, a case will be registered under the Prevention of Cruelty to Animals Act and the animal can be taken away and the owner jailed. And it will be a strong message to the neighbour that ill-treating animals is not allowed in your neighbourhood. If you don't know whom to contact, write me back and let me know where you live (city and state only) and I will get you the appropriate contact details.

It's monsoon, and my house and 5 dogs are crawling with ticks. Help!
Neena Parekh, Masjid Moth
Try 'Bayticol' liquid, manufactured by Bayer. It is for local application, to be dabbed along the spine from the neck to the base of the tail, with the help of a plastic dropper or a syringe with the needle removed. The animal should not be bathed for about a week after that. The effect should last for a month. However, now when you stroke the dog, please wash your hands afterwards.

Why is it that when there's something gross and smelly on the ground, dogs always seem to want to roll in it?
Ketan Fadnavis, Mehrauli
It is thought that this is a trait which harks back to the dogs' more wild relatives. Wolves are known to exhibit this behaviour, rolling in the carcasses or faeces of herbivores. It's believed that they do this in order to mask their scent and disguise themselves, thus increasing their chances of a successful sneak attack upon their prey. Then again, maybe, to a dog's way of thinking, it's just fun.

Do Rottweilers have violent instincts in them or does it depend on how they are raised?
Rottweilers were created and bred to be working dogs that were not too large. One of their normal chores was to keep an eye on children. They were bred to be strong, gentle, intelligent dogs who would be willing and able to work cooperatively with people. But inbreeding and bad breeding by people who believe that only those dogs with a fierce temperament should be allowed to live, have created some bloodlines and individuals who are less true to type. As a rule, no dog is born aggressive or negatively headstrong. Human error and foolishness accounts for most aggressive behaviours in animals, dogs included.

THE MOON IN THE WELL

Script Subba Rao
Illustrations Ram Waeerkar

ONE NIGHT A MAN WENT TO HIS WELL TO FETCH WATER.

OH GOD!

THE MOON HAS FALLEN INTO MY WELL!

I MUST TAKE HIM OUT AND THROW HIM BACK INTO THE SKY.

I'LL GET A HOOK AND A ROPE AND PULL HIM OUT.

AH! I'VE GOT HIM.

IN A MINUTE HE'LL BE OUT OF THE WELL AND UP IN THE SKY WHERE HE BELONGS.

PHEW! HE'S QUITE A HEAVY FELLOW!

THE MAN TUGGED AND TUGGED AT THE ROPE.

HE TUGGED SO HARD THAT THE HOOK GOT UNSTUCK.

THE MAN LOST HIS BALANCE AND FELL BACKWARDS.

HAH! SO I DID SUCCEED IN PUTTING YOU BACK UP THERE! YOU SHOULD BE GRATEFUL TO ME.

TINKLE PICTURE QUIZ

(I) Match the names of the following famous teachers (1 - 4) with their equally famous students (a - d).

1) Aristotle

2) Socrates

a) Plato

b) Arjuna

3) Dronacharya

4) Ramakrishna Paramahansa

c) Swami Vivekananda

d) Alexander

(II) Animals show some extraordinary behaviour patterns. Match the creatures (1 - 5) with their patterns of behaviour (a - e).

(1) Sea horse

(2) Puffer fish

(3) Sea cucumber

(4) Deep Sea Angler fish

a. I fill water in my body and swell up to scare off predators.
b. When someone threatens me, I shoot sticky, poisonous threads at them.
c. In my species, males store the eggs in their pouches and rear the young.
d. I use shock as a defence.
e. I dangle a light from my snout to attract tiny prey.

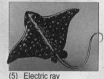

(5) Electric ray

(III) Match the names of the following sports (1 - 4) with the terms (a - d) associated with them.

1) Cricket
2) Lawn Tennis
3) Basketball
4) Football

a) Ace
b) Red Card
c) Leg Before Wicket
d) Dribbling

(IV) Match the following Nobel Prize winners (1 - 4) with their respective professions (a - d)

1) Amartya Sen

2) Mother Teresa

3) C. V. Raman

4) V. S. Naipaul

a) Social Worker   b) Economist   c) Writer   d) Physicist

Answers: (I) 1-d, 2-a, 3-b, 4-c   (III) 1-c, 2-a, 3-d, 4-b   (II) 1-c, 2-a, 3-b, 4-e, 5-d   (IV) 1-b, 2-a, 3-d, 4-c.

ANDROCLES AND THE LION

Script: Devanshu Mohapatra
Illustrations: Souren Roy

IN ANCIENT ROME, A SLAVE NAMED ANDROCLES, ONE DAY, RAN AWAY FROM HIS CRUEL MASTER.

HIS SOLDIERS WILL SOON BE AFTER ME. I MUST RUN AWAY AS FAR AS I CAN.

HE FLED INTO A JUNGLE...

...AND TOOK SHELTER IN A CAVE THERE.

SUDDENLY—

ROOOARR

A...A LION!

THIS MUST BE HIS CAVE! I'M TRAPPED!

?

HE'S HOLDING OUT HIS PAW... OH, THERE'S A THORN STUCK IN IT!

MY POOR FRIEND... HOW IT MUST PAIN YOU! LET ME TAKE IT OUT!

THERE!

AFTER ANDROCLES HAD TAKEN OUT THE THORN, THE LION QUIETLY WENT AWAY.

HE RETURNED AFTER A WHILE, WITH AN ANIMAL HE HAD CAUGHT.

OH, YOU'VE BROUGHT ME FOOD!

ANDROCLES STAYED WITH THE LION IN HIS CAVE. ONE DAY WHEN THE LION WAS AWAY —

SOLDIERS!

DON'T TRY TO RUN AWAY.

THE SOLDIERS TOOK ANDROCLES BACK TO HIS MASTER.

YOU KNOW HOW SLAVES WHO RUN AWAY ARE PUNISHED!

THROW HIM TO THE LIONS!

ONE OF THE PASTIMES OF THE ROMANS WAS TO WATCH FIGHTS BETWEEN MEN AND LIONS. THE FIGHTS USED TO TAKE PLACE IN A LARGE STADIUM CALLED THE ARENA.

SOME DAYS LATER, POOR ANDROCLES WAS PUSHED INTO ONE SUCH ARENA.

OUT YOU GO! LOOK AT THE CROWDS THAT HAVE COME TO SEE YOU.

IS THAT THE SLAVE! HE DOESN'T LOOK VERY STRONG TO ME.

LOOK, THEY'RE OPENING THE LION'S CAGE!

AS SOON AS THE CAGE WAS OPENED, THE LION RUSHED OUT.

THEY STARVED HIM FOR THREE DAYS. HE'LL TEAR THE SLAVE TO PIECES.

WHAT A HUGE CREATURE!

THE LION INDEED WAS VERY HUNGRY. HE RUSHED TOWARDS ANDROCLES.

ROOAR!

I HAVE NO CHANCE AGAINST THIS BEAST. BUT I WON'T RUN...

...I'LL STAND HERE AND FIGHT.

WHAT! HE DOESN'T WANT TO ATTACK!

COULD IT BE...? IS IT...?

IT IS YOU!

!

?

THIS IS AMAZING! THE FEROCIOUS LION HAS BECOME AS GENTLE AS A LAMB.

SO THEY CAUGHT YOU TOO. YOU HAVE BECOME SO LEAN. THEY HAVE BEEN STARVING YOU, HAVE THEY?

IT WAS THE SAME LION FROM WHOSE PAW ANDROCLES HAD REMOVED THE THORN!

THE CROWD WAS MOVED BY THE SCENE.

FREE THEM!

YES, LET THEM GO!

ANDROCLES AND THE LION WERE SET FREE. IT BECAME A COMMON SIGHT THEREAFTER TO SEE THE HUGE BEAST FOLLOWING ANDROCLES AROUND LIKE A SMALL PUPPY ON THE STREETS OF ROME.

THE SUN AND THE WIND

Script: Mohapatra
Illustrations: Ram Waeerkar

THE SUN AND THE WIND ONCE HAD A QUARREL.

I AM STRONGER THAN YOU.

WHO SAYS SO?

I CAN BLOW HUGE TREES AND HOUSES AWAY.

POOH! ANYONE CAN DO THAT.

CAN YOU MAKE THAT MAN TAKE OFF HIS SCARF? I BET YOU CAN'T.

CAN'T I? JUST WATCH.

WHOO

WHOOOOOOO

HEY, WHAT'S HAPPENING?

WHOOOOO

HELP!

BUT THE HARDER THE WIND BLEW THE TIGHTER THE MAN HELD ON TO HIS SCARF. FINALLY THE WIND GAVE UP.

THUMP

NO ONE COULD MAKE **THAT** FELLOW TAKE OFF HIS SCARF.

REALLY? MOVE ASIDE THEN, LET ME TRY.

THE SUN MADE HIMSELF VERY HOT.

WHAT NOW?

ONE MOMENT IT'S AS COLD AS WINTER.

THE NEXT MOMENT IT'S AS HOT AS SUMMER.

HE'S TAKEN OFF HIS SCARF.

I'D BETTER GO QUIETLY AWAY FROM HERE.

WELL, MY FRIEND...

...DO LET ME KNOW IF YOU WANT TO HAVE ANY MORE CONTESTS.

BUT THE WIND DIDN'T EVEN LOOK BACK. HE HAD HAD ENOUGH OF CONTESTS.

CRYBABY

When I was in LKG, I used to cry a lot and
everyone used to call me 'crybaby'.
One day, during the Onam festival, our
school had organised a cultural programme
and I was chosen to take part in a dance
performance. On the day of the programme,
when I went on stage and the music began
to play, I started crying loudly because
another participant had mistakenly stepped
on my foot. Everyone had a hearty laugh as
they watched me cry and dance at the same time.

— *Anjana Bhaktan,* Kochi, Kerala

THE COST OF A CHOCOLATE

When I was a little boy, I did not know the value
of money. Once, I took a 50-paise coin from my
mom's purse thinking it was ₹50 and went to
buy a bar of Dairy Milk chocolate. When I gave
the coin to the shopkeeper, he gave me the
chocolate without saying a word. On reaching
home, when mom saw the chocolate, she sent
me back to the shop to pay the remaining
amount.

— *Shruthi Shyam Somah,* Vikhroli, Mumbai

WHEN I MET UNCLE PAI

This incident took place years ago when I was sitting with my family in the waiting
lounge of the airport at Ahmedabad. While we were engrossed in reading a
newspaper, my mother suddenly spotted a person whose face she thought looked
familiar. She went straight to him and asked him whether he was Uncle Pai, the
Editor of *Tinkle* and *Amar Chitra Katha.* He replied in the
affirmative and my mother immediately called out to me
saying, "Look Maya, Uncle Pai is here." For a few
seconds, I stood stunned. It had always been my wish
to meet Uncle Pai in person and now I was right in front
of him. I quickly hugged him and touched his feet,
seeking his blessings. His wife, Mrs. Lalitha Pai, was
also with him. My joy knew no bounds and I just
couldn't believe that I was standing right in front of
Uncle Pai. I am sorry that today he is no more. May his
soul rest in peace.

— *Maya Shenoy,* Bengaluru

It Happened to Me!

ITALIAN COFFEE

One day, my parents were not at home and we had guests. They were tired and wanted a cup of coffee. I didn't know how to prepare it and instead of sugar, added salt to the brew. When the guests drank it, they liked it very much and asked me what it was. I told them it was Italian coffee. Now whenever they come home, they ask me to prepare Italian coffee for them!

— *Arusha Jain,* Alwar, Rajasthan

MONKEY MENACE

Once, my parents took me to Ayodhya. After offering our prayers at the temple, we went to bathe in the river. We were told to be very careful, as there were a lot of monkeys in the vicinity. When we entered the river, we took off our clothes and kept them aside. Later, we found the clothes missing. When we looked around, we saw a group of monkeys tearing at them with their teeth. We had to telephone mom who went back to the hotel and brought us another set of clothes.

— *Manish Ranjan,* Jhapatapur, West Bengal

WATER WOES

One day, I was thirsty and asked dad for a glass of water. He went to the fridge but found no water bottle there. But there was a bottle kept on the kitchen platform. Thinking that it contained water, he poured it into a tumbler and gave it to me. When I took a sip of the liquid, I found the taste funny and told dad about it. When he tasted it, he apologised for mistakenly giving me vinegar instead of water.

— *Pranaksh Chaudhary,* Andheri, Mumbai

TINKLE TELLS YOU WHY

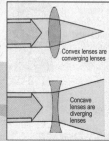

Convex lenses are converging lenses

Concave lenses are diverging lenses

Could you please explain the difference between a concave lens and a convex lens?
- K. Krithika, Chennai

A convex surface is a surface with a bulging curve like that on the outside of a ball, whereas a concave surface is a surface that sags inside, like the inside of a ball.

Convex lenses are converging lenses, i.e. the light rays passing through them come closer together.
Concave lenses are diverging lenses, i.e. the light rays passing through them spread out.

If moths are attracted to bright light how come they sleep during day time?
- A.V.S. Bhagyashree, Hyderabad

Every living animal or insect is either diurnal (i.e. active during day time) or nocturnal (active during night time). There is a set biological clock inherently present in the body of every animal and even in plants. Moths are nocturnal insects and thus they "sleep" during the day. Being inactive in the day also acts as a protection from predators. They mostly lie silently on tree trunks where they normally merge with the colour of the bark. Bright light however, from artificial sources attracts them It is a behaviour pattern.

THE GIANT ATLAS MOTH

What is the difference between a pirated and an original disc?
- Bikram Rabha, Guwahati, Assam

An original Video Cassette Disc (VCD) is the one sold by the producer or his agent, or the vendor who has purchased the disc from the producer. A pirated disc is a copy of a disc made without the permission or knowledge of the producer. It is like stolen property.

How do we find direction when we sail on the high seas?
- **Jane Jacob,** Mangalore, Karnataka

In ancient times, observing various celestial* bodies and constellations helped the sailors to navigate. Seasonal directions of the wind were also of some help. During the middle ages, navigators drew simple charts that included wind directions for different seasons, plus compass directions.

COMPASS

CHRONOMETER

Many of today's navigation instruments are the developed versions of the ones used earlier. The sextant, the chronometer and the compass are the basic instruments used in celestial navigation. While the compass gives the direction in which the ship is headed, the sextant helps in calculating the position of the ship with respect to those of a few stars. The chronometer gives the exact time to the second.

Using the information obtained, the exact position of a ship is calculated.

Apart from celestial navigation, sailors also use electronic devices that use radio signals for navigation. The Loran (Long Range Navigation), that uses low to medium-range frequency, Radar (Radio Detection and Ranging) and certain satellite systems are some of the instruments used in electronic navigation.

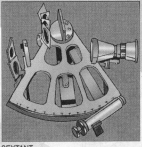

SEXTANT

* of the sky

THE TWO FARMERS

Story:
Shivnarayan Singh

Script:
Gayathri Chandrasekaran

Illustrations:
Prachi Killekar

RAMBHAU AND RATNAKAR WERE NEIGHBOURS. RAMBHAU WAS HARDWORKING WHILE RATNAKAR WAS LAZY.

RAMBHAU, WHY DO YOU WORK SO HARD? IT'S NOT LIKELY THAT GOLD WILL START GROWING ON YOUR TREES.

YOU NEVER KNOW...

...YOU SHOULD TILL YOUR LAND WELL. YOU WILL BE REWARDED FOR IT.

HA!

FOUR MONTHS LATER –

THE MANGO CROP IS EXCEPTIONALLY SWEET THIS YEAR. I MUST TAKE SOME FOR THE KING.

AND SO –

AH! WONDERFUL! YOU HAVE SLAVED THE ENTIRE YEAR TO PRODUCE THIS DELICIOUS FRUIT...

...I GIFT YOU A HUNDRED GOLD COINS.

THANK YOU, YOUR HIGHNESS!

WHEN RATNAKAR HEARD OF THE NEWS—

IF RAMBHAU CAN GET GOLD COINS FROM THE KING, SO CAN I. I MUST TAKE SOMETHING FOR THE KING BUT WHAT DO I TAKE?

HIS EYES FELL ON THE BULL THAT WAS TIED AT THE DOOR.

AH! I HAVE NO USE FOR YOU ANY MORE. YOU WILL GO TO THE KING AND FETCH ME A HUNDRED GOLD COINS.

AND—

YOUR HIGHNESS, YOU ARE A VERY GENEROUS KING. I HAVE BROUGHT YOU MY BULL AS A GIFT.

THANK YOU FOR THE BULL. HE WILL BE WELL TAKEN CARE OF IN MY PALACE. BUT I HAVE NOTHING TO OFFER YOU.

B...BUT....

THIS BULL HAS SERVED YOU WELL DURING ITS TIME BUT NOW THAT IT IS OLD AND WEAK YOU ARE GIVING IT AWAY. IS THAT THE RIGHT THING TO DO?

NO, YOUR HIGHNESS.

THEN, GO, MY GOOD MAN. WORK HARD AND YOU WILL GET ALL YOU WANT.

Anwar

SAVING ENERGY

Story
Prabha Nair

Script
Rajani Thindiath

Illustrator
Savio Mascarenhas

Colourist
Umesh Sarode

Letterer
Pranay Bendre

ANWAR'S CLASS TEACHER WAS TEACHING THE STUDENTS ABOUT CONSERVING ENERGY —

EACH OF US CAN MAKE A CONTRIBUTION IN OUR OWN WAY.

THIS IS YOUR HOMEWORK. WRITE DOWN ONE WAY IN WHICH YOU CAN SAVE ENERGY AT HOME.

NEXT MORNING —

ANWAR? ANWAR, GET UP. IT'S 7 O'CLOCK!

I'M NOT GOING...

ARE YOU ILL?

NO, I'M DOING MY HOMEWORK.

BY SLEEPING?

UH-HUH, BY SAVING ENERGY!

PROF. PANDU E. G. (Evil Genius)

Story — Basushankar Bharadwaj   Script — Rajani Thindiath   Art — Abhijeet Kini   Letters — Prasad Sawant

BOOM!

IT'S ALIIIIIIIIVE! HAHAHAHA!

GIRGIT! WHERE ARE YOU, LAZYBONES?

FRANKENSTEIN'S MONSTER WILL HAVE TO WAIT, FOR MY EMPLOYER, PROF. PANDU E. G., SURE WON'T! NO, HE'S NOT A REAL PROFESSOR.

HE WAS BADLY BULLIED AS A KID, SO HE DECIDED TO AVENGE THAT BY BECOMING AN EVIL SCIENTIST.

THAT'S THE E. G. AFTER HIS NAME, EVIL GENIUS!

HIS FAMILY HAS LEFT HIM RICHES SO HE CAN DO AS HE PLEASES. IS HE ANY GOOD?

ALAS, NO. GOGO, MY FRIEND, CATCHES THE BRUNT OF MOST OF HIS MISADVENTURES. OBVIOUSLY HE'S NOT TOO FOND OF THE PROF.

HE'S STARK, RAVING MAD!

NO, GOGO'S NOT A TALKING MONKEY. THE PROF TRIED A MIND CONTROL DEVICE ON HIM. ONLY IT WORKS AS A TRANSLATOR!
THERE YOU ARE, GIRGIT! WHERE'S THE NITROGLYCERINE?
YOU USED IT UP FOR THAT BETA RAY GUN.
AH, I FORGOT.
E.G.
IS THAT PURPLE STUFF DANGEROUS?
OF COURSE, IT IS! WHY DO YOU THINK I'M LOOKING FOR THE NITROGLYCERINE!
PROF, IS THAT SUPPOSED TO HAPPEN?
BLUB.. BLUB..
INTERESTING... ER... NO...
RUMBLE RUMBLE
GET DOWN, PROF!
NOTHING HAPPENED! THE RUMBLING'S STOPPED!
BURP!
PHEW! SO, IT WORKS WELL WITHOUT THE NITRO.